# Ballet Sisters

## THE NEWEST DANCER

# by Jan Ormerod

Cartwheel
B·O·O·K·S®

SCHOLASTIC INC.
New York   Toronto   London   Auckland   Sydney
Mexico City   New Delhi   Hong Kong   Buenos Aires

Copyright © 2008 by Jan Ormerod.
All rights reserved. Published by Scholastic Inc.
SCHOLASTIC, CARTWHEEL BOOKS, and associated logos are trademarks and/or registered trademarks of Scholastic Inc.

Library of Congress Cataloging-in-Publication Data

Ormerod, Jan.
Ballet sisters : the newest dancer / by Jan Ormerod.
p. cm.
"Cartwheel books."
Summary: Sylvie gets to attend ballet school, just like her big sister.
ISBN-13: 978-0-439-82282-4
ISBN-10: 0-439-82282-3
[1. Sisters--Fiction. 2. Ballet--Fiction. 3. Dancers--Fiction.] I. Title.
PZ7.O634Ban 2008
[E]--dc22                                              2007004378
ISBN-13: 978-0-439-82282-4
ISBN-10: 0-439-82282-3

10 9 8 7 6 5 4 3 2                                    8 9 10 11 12/0

Printed in Singapore
First printing, March 2008

# BALLET DAY

My name is Bonnie.

I love to dance.

Every Saturday, I go
to Miss Trisha's class.
My sister, Sylvie,
waits outside for me.

But Sylvie peeks in.

"Who is this?" says
Miss Trisha.

"This is my little sister," I say.

"Please," says Sylvie.

"I want to do ballet."

"Can you point your toes?"

says Miss Trisha.

Sylvie points her toes.

"Can you dance for me?"
I whisper, "Do your
ducky dance."

Sylvie does her ducky dance.

She waddles, flaps, and quacks.

"Very good," says
Miss Trisha. "Next week,
you can take class
with Miss Amy."

Sylvie and I skip
all the way home.

"Surprise," Mom says to Sylvie.

"This is your Not-Birthday."

"What is a Not-Birthday?"
Sylvie asks.

"It is not your birthday," I say.

"But you still get a card and
a present."

I help Sylvie open her present.

"It's for ballet," I tell her.

"A leotard, pink socks, and

ballet slippers.

And a pink sweater
I have grown out of.
All are just right
for Miss Amy's ballet class."

# THE NEWEST DANCER

The next Saturday,

I go to Miss Trisha's class.

Sylvie goes to
Miss Amy's class.

Sylvie learns naughty toes,

good toes, pointy toes,

and tippy toes.

Sylvie learns knee flaps,

knee bends,

and jump, jump, jump.

She learns pony trots
and rag dolls,

elephants and
butterflies.

Then the girls curtsy and
the boy bows.

Miss Amy says, "Well done, dancers. And well done to our newest dancer, Sylvie."

At home, Sylvie and I
dress up.

"I am a swan," Sylvie says.

"Me, too," I say.

And we dance together.